About the Book

A once idyllic meadow, home to animals, birds, insects, wildflowers and ancient apple trees, is clear cut to make way for new construction.
Miraculously there is one survivor...a lonely little dandelion.

When her golden petals turn to white fluff, she takes flight in search of a new home. We get a bird's eye view of her journey over many big houses and manicured green lawns, and when she spots a lush green meadow, surrounded by wetlands, we follow her down to earth, and cheer as she puts down new roots.

We meet all the inhabitants of this small family farm, and observe their daily life.

What's special about this family is that each of their activities contribute to a sustainable lifestyle, and consequently lead to a brighter and more promising future.

A contemporary environmental fable that is as informative as it is timely.
Young readers, as well as parents and teachers, can explore many earth friendly techniques, including organic gardening, solar and wind power, water harvesting and alternative heating, as well as growing medicinal herbs and cultivating gourmet mushrooms on logs.

There is a Glossary, and family friendly ideas for Cooking with Dandelions.
An informative Resource List of follow up links encourages readers to further explore these green techniques.

THE RUNAWAY DANDELION

by Jill Regensburg

Illustrations by Leticia Plate

Once there was a beautiful meadow filled with wildflowers. There were dandelions, buttercups, Johnny-jump-ups, black eyed Susans, Queen Ann's lace, wild lavender, and lots and lots of sweet purple clover.

Wild blueberries and strawberries grew everywhere and there were many ancient apple trees.

The meadow was alive with bumble bees, birds of every color, butterflies, deer, rabbits and field mice.

All of these creatures considered this lovely meadow their home. They lived in the trees, the tall grasses that danced gracefully when the gentle breezes blew, and in holes in the rich brown earth. These happy creatures were content to spend their days gathering nuts and berries, catching bugs, sipping dew drops, or just relaxing in the warm sunshine.

One day some very large machines arrived and in no time, had cut down the ancient apple trees, torn up the graceful grasses, flowers and berries, and frightened all the creatures from their beloved home.

Then some humans came,
and built a very large
house right in the middle
of what used to be the
beautiful meadow.

After the house was built,
some other humans
arrived and planted a
big lawn around the new
house.

When the new grass grew in, there were also many pretty yellow
dandelions, which broke up the monotony of the big green
lawn and made it sparkle.

But, along came another machine spraying chemicals all over the lawn to get rid of the dandelions. These nasty chemicals also killed all the ladybugs, grasshoppers, crickets, and other insects that had taken up residence in the new lawn.

Miraculously, one little dandelion survived.

Realizing that she was alone, the dandelion became quite sad and longed for some company. A bumblebee perhaps, to tickle her yellow petals while gathering pollen to take back to its hive to make honey.

Or, a hummingbird in search of a sip of sweet nectar. Even a spider, looking for a likely spot to spin its web, would have been welcome company.

But none of these creatures came because their sensitive antennae warned them that the chemicals on the lawn were not anything they wanted to get close to.

So the lonely little dandelion
spent her days in sadness.

One day, the little dandelion noticed that her beautiful yellow petals had turned to white fluff, and when a gust of wind happened by, the white fluff lifted her off her stem and up into the air. This fluff had dandelion seeds attached to it, and suddenly she found herself drifting along in the breeze, up above the green lawn and over the big house.

The wind carried her quite a long way and all the while she was looking for a new place to settle down.

For a long time, all she could see were
more green lawns and more big houses.

At last she looked down and spied a lovely meadow, where colorful wildflowers, berries, fruit and nut trees were growing.

Birds were singing, insects buzzing, and lots of animals scurried about. There was a pond, and lush wetlands, where water plants thrived and a Great Blue Heron fished for his breakfast. There was also a big organic vegetable garden.

15

Nearby was a house that was different from the ones she had seen. For one thing, it wasn't very big.

Instead of getting electricity from wires, coming in from a power plant, this little house used the sunshine and wind to make all the electricity it needed with solar panels on the roof and a wind turbine nearby.

Rain barrels collected water, falling from the tin roof, to use for drinking, washing, and watering plants that grew in an attached glass greenhouse.

Surrounding all of this was a dense green forest where a
team of large horses was helping a man clear out the dead
trees to cut up for firewood.

The dandelion knew that this was the kind of home she had been searching for, so she drifted slowly down to earth, and settled herself right next to the pond.

She immediately began sprouting her roots down into the moist soil, where she was soon greeted by some friendly earthworms and nematodes, who had conveniently aerated the soil so as to make it easier for her to put down her roots.

Once settled, she looked around to see chickens, ducks and geese pecking around in the garden, eating the weeds and bugs and fertilizing the soil as they went.

Soon some children, carrying baskets, came
into the garden and began to pick vegetables
that were planted in groups called "families".
This helped the plants grow strong and healthy.

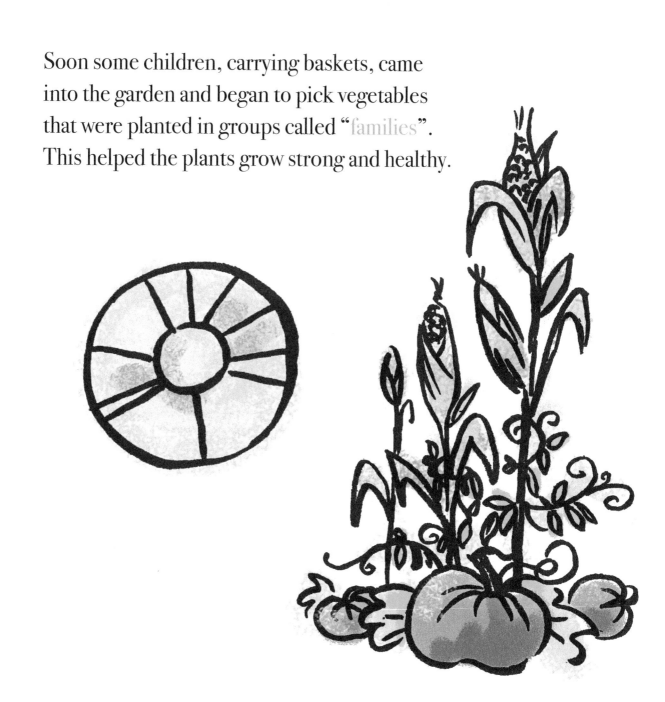

They laughed and sang as they gathered fruit, nuts and berries from the nearby trees and bushes.

When their baskets were full, they carried them back to the out-door kitchen where they helped their mom make them into delicious pies and jams, or freeze them to save for the following winter.

After awhile, the little dandelion noticed that when the children weren't busy in the garden, planting, harvesting or mulching, they were happily grooming the horses, collecting fresh eggs from the chicken house and looking after all the animals that shared their farm.

On hot summer days, they couldn't wait to swim in their Natural Swimming Pool, where a tire swing dangled from a thick rope. The kids spent many happy hours swinging way out, bellowing like Tarzan and Jane of the Jungle, and leaping into the cool water.

They even made their own fishing poles to catch fish that their dad would be waiting to cook in an outdoor stone oven, when they returned hungry from the pond.

He also baked bread and pizza and they would help him knead the dough. Their favorite part was punching the dough down after it had risen.

They also had a tree house which they had helped to build, and loved to hide in and have secret meetings with their friends, who visited from nearby farms.

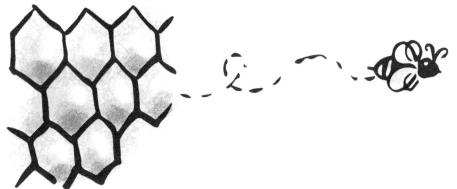

The little dandelion noticed that the children hardly ever had time to watch TV, since they were having too much fun collecting honeycombs from the beehives they tended, or having contests to see who could build the tallest pile of firewood for the wood stove that kept the little house warm and cozy in winter.

They were glad they didn't have to mow the lawn because instead of grass it was planted with edible herbs and flowers.
Nearby, in the cool, damp forest, their dad picked mushrooms that he cultivated on fallen logs.

In the early spring, the whole family worked together to collect the buckets of sap from their large grove of maple trees.

They put the buckets in a big wagon that the horses pulled to the nearby sugaring house, where it cooked for many hours over hot coals, spewing out steam and boiling down into delicious, thick maple syrup.

They enjoyed the maple syrup on their pancakes and on the snow cones they loved to make in winter. They also helped to sell jugs of it in summer, at the local farmers market, along with baskets of their mushrooms and the organic produce from their garden.

For a special treat they camped overnight in a tipi that their parents had built and lived in, long ago, while they were building their little house.

On rainy days they helped their dad work on an old truck that he was converting to run on biofuel instead of gasoline. This was made from corn that he grew on the farm.

One spring day their mom was making lunch and sent them to her Spiral herb garden to pick some fresh basil, parsley and cilantro for the salad of micro greens that she grew in the greenhouse.

She also grew medicinal herbs and flowers that she made into tinctures to use when one of them was not feeling well.

Next to the pond the kids shouted,
"Hey, look at all these beautiful dandelions!
Let's pick some of their yummy green leaves to add to the salad!".

The little dandelion smiled up at them.
She wasn't lonely any more.

COOKING WITH DANDELIONS

When cooking with the flowers they are best picked in early Spring or Fall when they are fully open and dry, in an area where they have not been sprayed with chemicals and have not been near any traffic. Rinse carefully to remove any grit or bugs and remove the stems. Squeeze the tips of each flower between your fingers, and with your other hand, pinch the green base of the flower until the petals are released into a bowl.

Fresh dandelion flowers are a great addition to your favorite cookie recipes (oatmeal or lemon cookies work the best). Some other great things to add dandelion flowers to are: pasta, pizza, rice, pesto, oatmeal, ice cream, sorbet, jams and jellies, lemonade and iced tea.

When cooking with the leaves (called greens), they are best picked when young and tender. They can be eaten raw, mixed with other lettuces and herbs in salads, or sautéed with onions, garlic and wild mushrooms. They make a great addition to pizza, pasta, pesto, chili, omelettes, quiches, frittatas, and soups.

My favorite dandelion recipe is Dandelion Fritters! These are easy and fun to make! You can find the recipe at: www.learningherbs.com/remedies-recipes/dandelion-fritters.

Have FUN cooking TOGETHER!

GLOSSARY

Aerated – Fluffing up the soil to add air to it so plants will grow better

Biofuel – made from plants such as corn and used instead of gasoline

Converting – changing over to something different

Cultivated – Getting the soil ready to plant seeds by turning over, fertilizing, mulching, watering

Edible – Safe to eat

Harvesting – Picking

Medicinal – Helps to cure

Micro Greens – Young plants

Mulching – Covering plants with leaves, wood chips or straw to discourage weeds and protect from freezing

Natural Swimming Pool - A pool that has no chemicals that uses native plants and layers of sand and rock to filter impurities

Nematode – Tiny worms that eat soil pests

Organic - Natural; produced without chemicals

Plant Families – Combining plants that help each other grow

Solar Panels – Metal and glass frames that collect heat from the sun to create electricity

Spiral Herb Garden – A design for growing lots of herbs in a small vertical space

Tinctures – Creating healing liquids from herbs and flowers

Wetlands – Swamps or bogs that fill up with rainwater where wildlife thrive

Wind Turbine – A Tall pole with metal blades at top that are rotated by the wind to create electricity

Permaculture – All of the techniques in this book are practiced in Permaculture (permanent agriculture), a system of designing and creating indoor and outdoor spaces that mirror nature and are organic and sustainable.

Resources & Links to Useful Websites

Permaculture Design Magazine
http://www.permacultureprincipals.com
http://www.jamiesfoodrevolution.org
http://www.edibleschoolyard.com
http://www.letsmove.gov
The Power of Permaculture – Ryan Harb – Tedx Utica
http://www.urbanhomestead.org
http://www.1000ecofarms.com
http://www.smallplanet.org
http://www.treehuggers.com
http://www.nofamass.org
http://www.thesolutionsproject.org
http://www.billmckibben.com
http://www.peta.org
http://www.meatfreemondays.com
http://www.Energy.Gov   Active solar Heating
                               Wood and Pellet heating
http://www.motherearthnews.com How to Build a Natural Swimming Pool
                                How to Bake Using an Earth Oven
http://www.modernfarmer.com
Raising Backyard Chickens for Dummies
https://www.youtube.com/user/JamieOliver
http://www.transitionus.org

About the Author

As a Certified Permaculture Designer, the author's focus is on creating sustainable, organic indoor and outdoor spaces for living and growing food. She has designed and, for many years, lived on a homestead in Vermont, such as described in the story.

As a Natural Foods Personal Chef and teacher she is passionate about preparing and eating organic, local, seasonal food and embracing an earth friendly lifestyle.

As a mother and grandmother, she believes that inspiring young students to embrace ecologically sound environmental practices is the key to saving Planet Earth.

The author's practice of Permaculture (Permanent-Agriculture) takes its cues from, and imitates Nature. The tenacity of her little dandelion "guru" inspired this contemporary fable. Who knew that something as common, unassuming and often despised, as a dandelion would have so many lessons to teach, as well as being a role model for students of all ages?

About the Illustrator

Leticia Plate was born in Buenos Aires, Argentina and grew up in Rome, Italy. A graduate of School of Visual Arts in NYC, her work has been published in various magazines & national newspapers. She now lives in Portland, Maine with her family, a sweet dog and three temperamental chickens.
Her work can be seen at www.leticiaplate.com

CPSIA information can be obtained
at www.ICGtesting.com
Printed in the USA
FSOW04n0525151117
40958FS